This book presents an easy and effective approach to learning to manage angry feelings. Children are encouraged to acknowledge their angry feelings and identify the triggers, cope with the physical arousal caused by anger (calm their body), cope with the mental experience of anger (calm their mind and think helpful thoughts), and to process and learn from their experience. These steps empower them to make a different decision in the future or reward themselves for making a good decision in the present. Children also learn in this book that the key to success is to practice this method as a way to continually learn about themselves, what personal and environmental experiences upset them, and how they can make the best decisions for their own emotional health and wellbeing.

Through helpful narrative and examples, children and parents will learn strategies to talk to themselves and each other about anger, to normalize its expression, and to manage angry feelings effectively using healthy coping strategies.

Emotions make a difference,
In how a day can go.
The more you learn about them,
The more that you can grow.

No matter what you have in life,
How great that you may be...
Anger turns things upside down,
And upsets us easily.

It brews within your belly,
Starts an itching in your nose.
It heats you up from inside out,
And flushes down your toes.

You may not understand it,
The discomfort that you feel.
But you should not ignore it,
For it won't remain concealed.

Anger's a reaction,
That is normal when it comes.
Like all emotions, healthy,
For you'd rather not be numb.

Yet, when it's unacknowledged,
It can fester like a cut...
Impacting what you say and do,
While oozing in your gut.

Every day you're getting older,
Interacting with the world.
Facing challenges that come your way,
Like every boy and girl.

Though some battles are external,
There are those you fight within.
And controlling how you react,
Is a battle you can win.

One thing you can control in life,
Is how you view each day.
Not only what you say and do,
But how you pave the way.

When anger rears its sizzling head,
Ask: How will you react?
How can you voice the way you feel,
But hold back from an attack?

Maybe you feel angry,
That your sister stole your treat.
You spilled your juice all down your shirt,
Or tripped on tangled feet.

You lost the game you tried to win,
Your best friend left you out...
These things can fizz beneath your skin,
Causing chaos all about.

Perhaps you're feeling angry,
That you have to go to school...
It's cold or hot, you'd rather not,
You hate that silly rule.

No matter what the reason is,
Your anger's there – it's real.
And once you say "hello" to it,
You can manage how you feel.

STEP

1

Acknowledge the emotion,
Use your words to give it voice...
"Although I'm feeling angry,
My reaction is my choice."

Name the source of your frustration,
Use your words and not your hands.
Tell your Mom, or Dad, or teacher,
Find someone who understands.

STEP

2

Count your breaths for one whole minute,
Slowly in, and slowly out.
It's okay to step away,
Be alone if you're in doubt.

Take a moment by yourself,
Until your head feels clear.
Don't yell or stomp, but ask yourself,
Am I still in high gear?

There's calm in repetition,
So let's choose a phrase for you...
"I am stronger than my anger,"
Or, "I'm Okay" will do.

Repeat it and repeat it,
Until your rage subsides...
Drop your shoulders from your ears,
Find calm from deep inside.

STEP

4

Replay the situation,
Understand what made you mad.
How could you do things differently,
What made you feel so bad?

If you had superpowers,
Then what would you do right now?
Say something nice, clean up your toys,
Or change the world somehow!

It's important to remember,
That it's normal to feel things.
Emotions form our bonds with life,
They make us cry or sing.

Even anger is productive,
An opportunity to ask...
"How can I do things better?"
It's a test you're bound to pass.

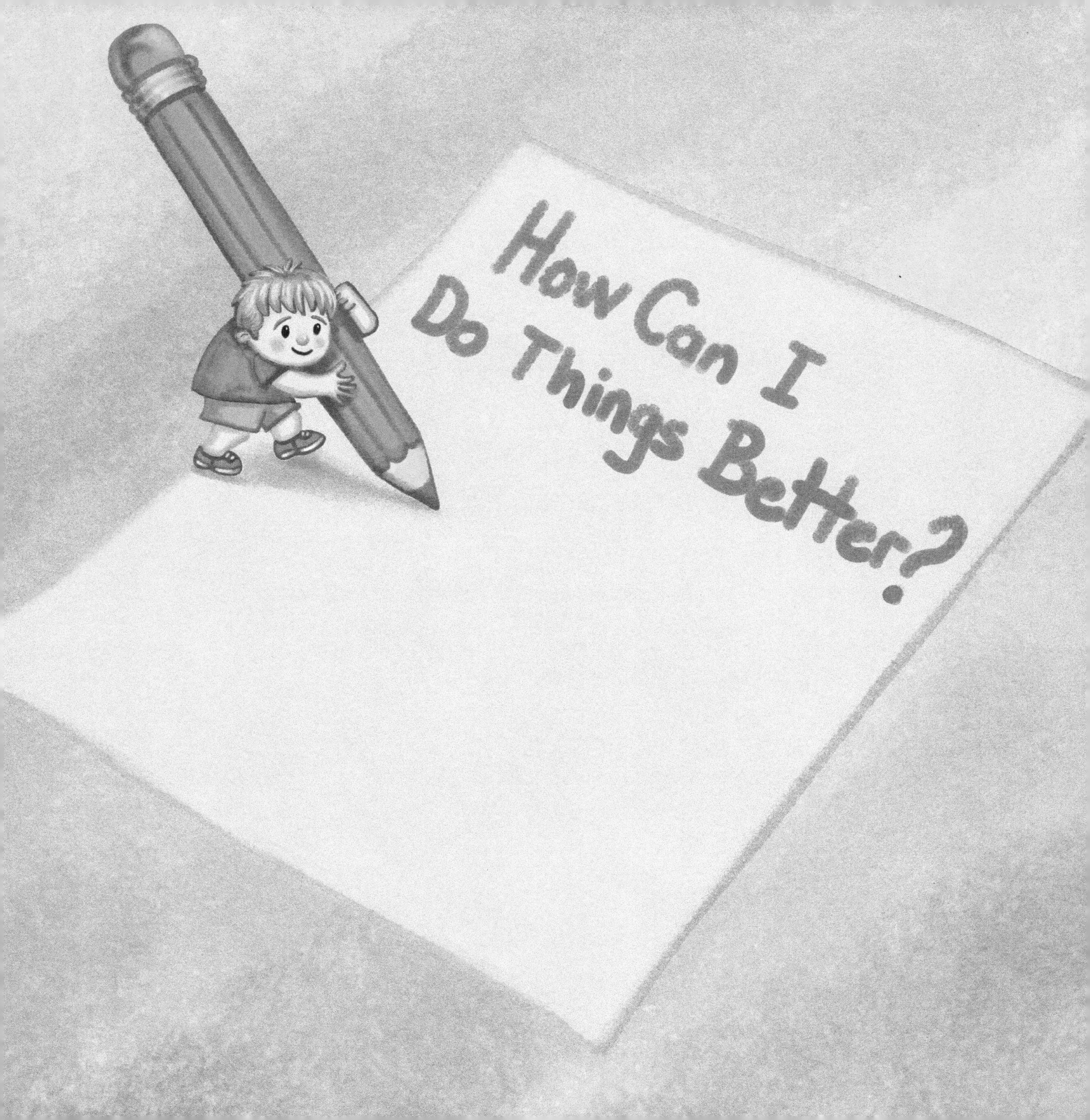
How Can I
Do Things Better?

Like every sport we practice,
We can't just jump in the game.
You have to learn the smaller skills,
As no moment is the same.

But the more that you encounter,
Situations that are tough...
And practice your reactions,
You'll soon be calm enough.

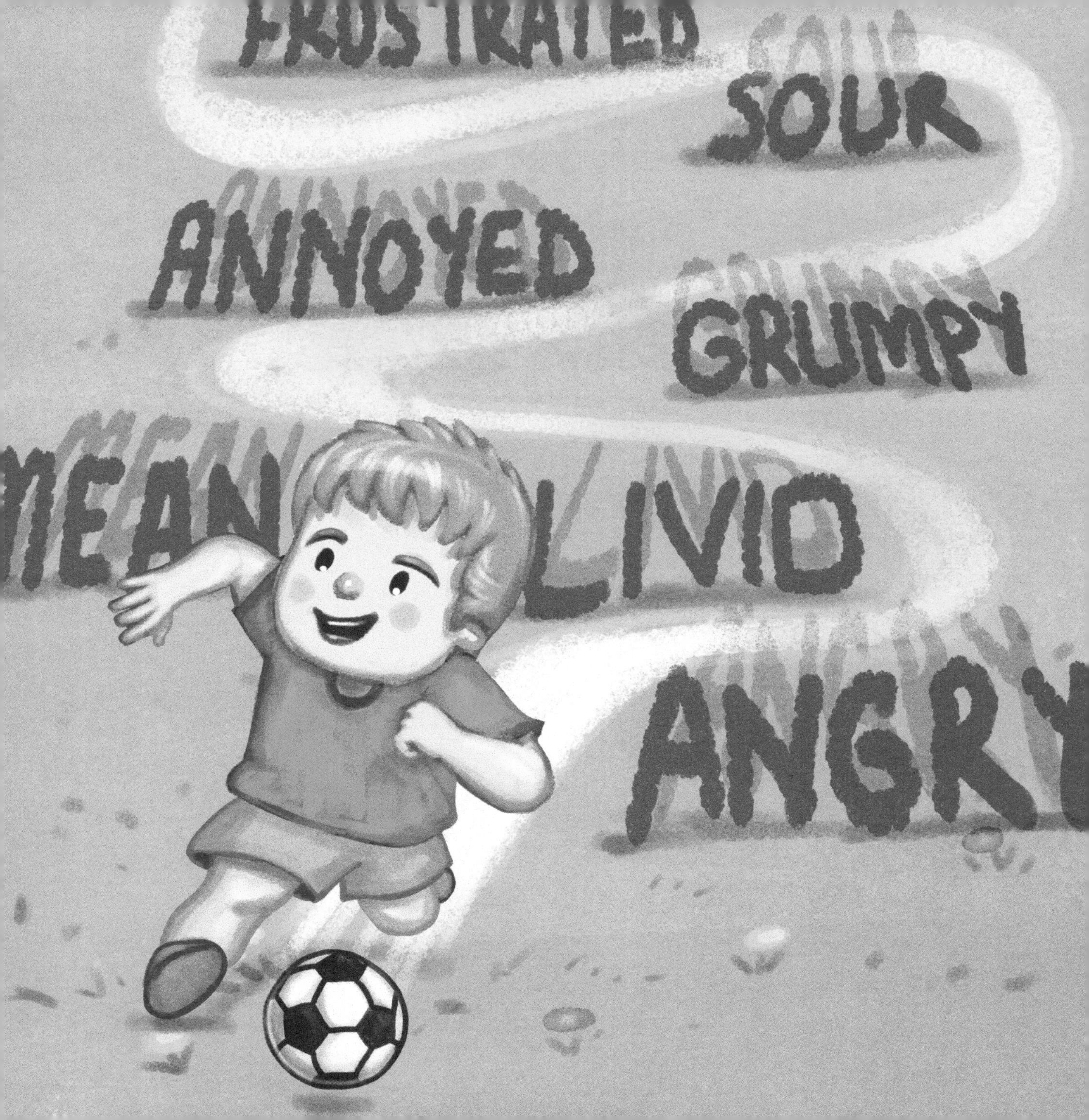
FRUSTRATED
SOUR
ANNOYED
GRUMPY
MEAN
LIVID
ANGRY

You'll notice that these feelings,
Are less frightening with time.
Like summiting a mountain,
Things seem smaller as you climb.

Feelings are a superpower,
That you can tend and grow.
Practice hard, you'll have it too,
You're stronger than you know!

Claim your FREE Gift!

 Visit:

PDICBooks.com/Gift

Thank you for purchasing

Today, I Feel...

Angry

and welcome to the Puppy Dogs & Ice Cream family.
We're certain you're going to love the little gift
we've prepared for you at the website above.

CPSIA information can be obtained
at www.ICGtesting.com
Printed in the USA
LVHW071445190323
741977LV00034B/532

9 781957 922607